MEET ALL THESE FRIENDS IN BUZZ BOOKS:

Thomas the Tank Engine
The Animals of Farthing Wood
Winnie-the-Pooh
Fireman Sam
Joshua Jones
Rupert
Babar

First published in Great Britain in 1995
by Buzz Books
an imprint of Reed Children's Books
Michelin House, 81 Fulham Road, London SW3 6RB
and Auckland, Melbourne, Singapore and Toronto

ISBN 1 85591 4417

Printed in Italy by Olivotto

ENTER THE RAT

Story by Norman Redfern
Illustrations by Arkadia

It was a dark night in Chicago. The Mayor was working late at City Hall when three gangsters burst in.

"What is the meaning of this?" he demanded.

"The meanin' of this is that you're comin' for a little ride!" grunted Greasepit, dragging him away.

Throttle, Vinnie and Modo were in their scoreboard hang-out at Quigley Field. They were playing basketball with the radio turned up loud. Charley stormed in and pulled the plug.

"We were jamming to that!" protested Vinnie.

"Not any more!" said Charley. "The Mayor's been kidnapped!"

"This could make me mad!" said Modo.

7

"That's not all," said Charley. "Guess which overripe cheese has taken over as Mayor?"

"Limburger!" said Throttle.

"Now I *am* mad!" said Modo.

There were big changes at City Hall. Limburger had taken over the Mayor's office, and Karbunkle had built a laboratory upstairs. And the new Mayor had a new secretary.

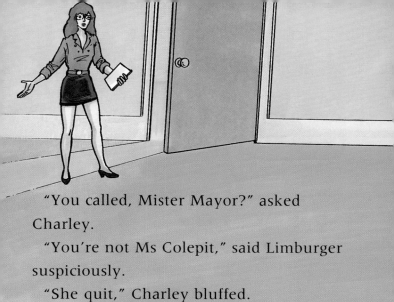

"You called, Mister Mayor?" asked Charley.

"You're not Ms Colepit," said Limburger suspiciously.

"She quit," Charley bluffed.

She hoped that her disguise would fool Limburger – at least until she had uncovered his latest evil plan.

"Take a memo," said Limburger. "In order to assist construction of the new subway system, the Diamond Exchange will be demolished – immediately!"

"But there are people in there!" protested Charley.

"I'm the Mayor now," snorted Limburger. "Chicago is all mine!"

That night, the Plutarkian demolition
squad knocked down the Diamond
Exchange. People ran for their lives as
rubble crashed around them. Diamonds
worth millions of dollars spilled into the
street.

Limburger's men drove their giant
vacuum truck into the mound of
diamonds and filled up its tank with
precious gems.

11

Suddenly, three powerful motorbikes roared into life. The Biker Mice From Mars soared over the edge of a tall building and landed in front of the villains.

"Hey there!" shouted Throttle. "You're destroying property."

"And endangering people," added Vinnie.

"And that makes us really mad!" concluded Modo.

The Biker Mice From Mars drew their weapons, but the thieves were in no mood to fight. The vacuum truck screeched away in a cloud of dust.

Throttle bent down and picked up a handful of diamonds.

"Why would Limburger steal a truckload of diamonds?" he wondered.

"He doesn't need the money," Vinnie pointed out.

"It's a mystery, all right," Throttle nodded, "and I've got a feeling we won't like the answer!"

At that very moment, in the Mayor's office, Limburger was putting the finishing touches to his plan.

"I shall dig up the entire city of Chicago and deliver it personally to the Plutarkian High Chairman," he boasted. "That will knock his smelly socks off!"

"Now, Karbunkle," he went on, "is my Digging Machine ready yet?"

"Almost," hissed Karbunkle, punching a button on his control panel.

"May I introduce the driver? Behold – the Tunnel Ratt!"

The transporter chamber crackled fiercely. Inside it, Limburger could see a gigantic, evil-looking rat!

"Not another mouse!" he groaned.
Tunnel Ratt aimed his laser jackhammer at an ornate column. He blasted at it furiously, carving a statue of Throttle out of the marble.

16

"*That's* a mouse," said Tunnel Ratt. "I'm a rat. I eat mice for breakfast."

"I like him!" chuckled Limburger.

Next day, Charley had more news for the Biker Mice From Mars.

"Whatever Limburger's up to, it's going to happen soon," she told them. "He's building something big at a secret factory just outside town!"

"Come on, bro's," yelled Throttle. "Time to rock –"

"– and ride!" added Vinnie and Modo.

In a secret factory in a deserted part of town, the massive Digging Machine, was ready for action. Its enormous drill, covered with truck-loads of stolen diamonds, sparkled in the factory floodlights.

"Impressive," smiled Limburger, "but is it big enough?"

"Big enough to strip-mine all Chicago in a single day," hissed Karbunkle.

"Good," smiled Limburger, "because this time tomorrow, the Windy City will be gone with the wind!"

Limburger and Karbunkle climbed aboard the Digging Machine. Tunnel Ratt was at the controls, and in the corner, tied up, was the kidnapped Mayor.

"Ready to dig, Mister Big!" laughed Tunnel Ratt.

"Then let's do it!" ordered Limburger.

The Biker Mice From Mars skidded to a
halt outside Limburger's secret factory.
Modo's laser-cannon burned a porthole
through the concrete wall.

Throttle, Vinnie, Modo and Charley
watched as the Digging Machine's
diamond-studded drill cut through the
solid ground beneath Chicago.

20

"Looks like Limburger's finally gettin' into heavy rock," growled Modo.

"Which means we've got to roll!" said Throttle. "Grab those leftover diamonds and follow me!"

Back at the Last Chance Garage, Charley fitted diamond-covered cones to the front of their bikes. Then they roared off to stop Limburger destroying Chicago.

Ahead of them, there was an ominous
rumble, and a derelict building collapsed.
The Digging Machine was at work
beneath the city streets!

"Time for the concrete test!" yelled
Vinnie.

"You got it! Blast off!" shouted Modo.

They jumped their bikes into the air,
then dived nose-first towards the street.

Their new diamond-tipped cones drilled into the concrete. They were on their way underground!

"Why don't we take the short-cut, guys?" asked Modo.

He took Throttle and Vinnie deeper and deeper into the earth. Suddenly, they smashed through into an open tunnel.

"Wow! The subway! Rock and rail!"
grinned Vinnie.

They roared through the tunnel and
blasted up into the rock ahead of
Limburger's digging machine. Then they
waited, their bikes, headlights blazing, in
full Battle Mode.

24

"It's those wretched rodents!" stormed
Limburger. "Take care of them!"

"Gladly," said Tunnel Ratt. "I tear
meeces to pieces!"

Tunnel Ratt jumped aboard his high-
speed mining cart and charged towards
the Biker Mice.

"Time to burrow, bro's!" said Throttle.

They crashed through the rock,
swerving crazily to dodge Tunnel Ratt's
laser blasts.

Karbunkle and Limburger watched the chase on the digging machine's radar.

"The Ratt has those Mice trapped!" gloated Karbunkle.

Limburger wasn't so sure.

"Look!" he said. "They've changed course. They're coming right at us!"

A split second before they reached the machine, the Biker Mice changed direction again. Tunnel Ratt wasn't quick enough. He crashed through the side of the machine and smashed into the main power unit.

26

"Malfunction! The controls are dead!" shouted Karbunkle.

"But I must have control," said Limburger. "I'm the Mayor!"

"Not any longer, Limburger," said Throttle. "Your days as Head Cheese are over!"

Vinnie smashed into the control room and rescued the real Mayor of Chicago.

"It's an honour, your Honour!" he joked.

Throttle, Vinnie and Modo escorted the Mayor back to City Hall.

"You didn't just save my life," said the Mayor, "you saved the city, too. I must reward you..."

The Mayor checked his pockets.

"Oh dear," he said, "all I seem to have with me are some vouchers for free hot dogs and root beer."

He looked anxiously at his rescuers, but their faces were hidden behind their helmet visors.

"You got a deal!" said the Biker Mice From Mars. "Ride free, Citizen!"